# Romance

# In a

# Garage

# Romance

# In a

# Garage

## Leroy Vincent

Copyright © 2020. All rights reserved.

No part of this publication may be reproduced, stored in a retrieval system or transmitted in any way by any means, electronic, mechanical, photocopy, recording or otherwise, without the prior permission of the author except as provided by USA copyright law.

All characters appearing in this work are fictitious. Any resemblance to real persons, living or dead, is purely coincidental.

The opinions expressed by the author are not necessarily those of Publisher.

Book design Copyright © 2020. All rights reserved.

RWG Publishing
PO Box 596
Litchfield, IL 62056
https://rwgpublishing.com/

Published in the United States of America

Daniel Carter wakes up to the electronic screech of his alarm clock. The room is dark, and Daniel is almost tempted to stay in bed a little longer. The embrace of sleep still close. Luckily for him, the alarm he bought makes a particularly piercing and annoying noise, and it's pushed just out of reach on Daniel's bedside table. Both the purchasing of such an annoying clock and the placing of it were strategic choices for Daniel.

He's always had a hard getting up early, but his day is full, and the time is needed. Daniel pushes himself out of bed, moving the covers aside as he turns the alarm off. In the silence, Daniel checks the display of the clock. It reads 6.00 am, and for a minute he almost curses, irritated that he has to get at this time every morning, but after all, he has a business to run.

Daniel owns a garage on the outskirts of his small town, and between setting up shop, organizing everything for a day's work, and early visits from customers, an early start is exactly what's needed. Daniel remembers how people reacted when he first said he was going to make a move to buy the garage.

He had worked there for years under the previous owner, and when they fell ill and had to retire, he saw it as a natural choice to buy it. After all, Daniel had an insider's knowledge of the garage, of how it all worked, and the one thing he couldn't make peace with was the idea of a stranger taking over the responsibility of running a business they had no real interest in.

Still, most of Daniel's friends thought he was crazy at the time, and some couldn't understand how he could work in the garage day in and day out, but the truth is that he loved it. The work felt honest, and working with his hands seemed to act as a source of clarity for Daniel.

It was as if his head cleared as his body worked, and he could truly think. He loved everything about his work, how physical it was, the smell of the oil, even the dirty marks on his skin, and overalls because they all signaled another day of hard and honest work.

As he shaves in the bathroom sink, Daniel smiles as he thinks back to the day he signed the paperwork that made the garage his, how even his sister said he'd be better off thinking about retirement, and that was almost ten years ago.

Daniel looks at himself in the mirror, wiping the last of the shaving cream from his chin. He's an attractive man, and at 43, his age seems to complement his already handsome features. His black hair is peppered with flecks of grey hairs here and there, and his eyes are strong yet kind. His love of physical work has helped him stay in good shape, and his skin sports a healthy glow as a result. As Daniel sets about his daily routine of setting up shop he wonders idly what the day has in store for him.

Rachel Wallace is not having a good day. After another mind-numbing board meeting which she wishes she could forget, her assistant messed up her coffee order, and brought her some soy latte.

The sharp, sour taste was so bad Rachel wanted to spit it out, but she knew that would be a bit dramatic. That didn't stop her from chewing out her assistant, though.

Honestly, she even felt awkward doing that, especially with how embarrassed he looked already. Her assistant was hired just out of college, and he was on the young side, so Rachel practically felt like his mother or a strict teacher, giving him a scolding. What added to this feeling was the fact that Rachel was 45, and almost exclusively dressed in formal wear.

Of course, she had to dress to impress for work; when you work as a financial advisor, the image can sometimes be everything. Rachel was good at what she did and paid well for it, which was helpful since she often had to spend outlandish sums of money to get a new suit, or on a fancy dinner to impress clients.

Rachel's world was high stress, but she handled it with grace. While others saw working in the financial sector as a shortcut to premature bald spots, Rachel was more than capable of keeping her cool.

She knew her skills and abilities and trusted in them, knowing that even if a project or deadline was just around the corner she could manage it. Rachel had seen the stress of her job get to others though. She had seen a worker turn from wide-eyed and energetic into a ball of stress, chugging coffee like it was oxygen. Rachel had a special routine to help her reduce stress, and this involved a mix of pilates, yoga, gym visits, and mindfulness meditation.

She took care of her body, and it returned the favor, helping her maintain a healthy look and a full head of hair too. Too put it simply Rachel was blessed with beauty and had been known to turn a few heads in the office. Although she tries to keep her distance from that kind of thing, Rachel knew that the rumor mill spun in her office, and often it would raise rumors about whether or not she was 'involved' with any of the clients or other workers from the firm.

However, Rachel mostly kept to herself when it came to dating. It's not that there wasn't anyone interested in her; in fact, more than a few times when she was supposed to be wining and dining a potential client the client would try and make a pass at her, asking to meet 'outside of work' at a more 'cozy' restaurant or bar. Of course, Rachel wasn't so gullible and knew these men were looking for a one-night stand to brag about back home.

Rachel had decided long ago that she would only go for the right man when she found him.

She left a lot of this up to fate, but she knew someone from the financial world would most likely be the best fit.

Rachel was having a bad day already, but her car just decided to make things worse. As she was driving along the road to her favorite lunch spot, her vehicle began to make a worrying noise. It sounded like a stuttering cough, like the car itself had the beginnings of a cold.

Rachel frowned as she tried to locate the source of the noise, seeing if she could do anything to soothe or stop it. But the sound just escalated as she drove along until it filled the whole car. What made it worse was that the car started to shudder and shake unusually, rocking Rachel in her chair.

Rachel could take a hint when she got one and started to look out the window, her eye-catching the sign for a garage up the road. Just as she pulled in her car made a very worrying squealing noise, before shuddering to a stop.

Rachel let out an exasperated sigh, her day officially ruined, and as she walked into the front room, she couldn't help but frown. This garage was messy, with old oil rags on the countertops, faded posters on the wall, and worn tires stacked in the corner of the room haphazardly.

With a slight feeling of uneasiness, Rachel rang the little bell that had been set on the counter to get the attention of whichever worker may be here. Daniel had been in the back of the garage, working on a passion project of his, the restoration of an old, nearly obsolete engine. When he heard the bell, he hurried out and was met with a beautiful woman, well-dressed and looking slightly impatient. "Hello, I'm Daniel, but you can call me Danny, what can I do for you?" Daniel takes the woman's hand and shakes it warmly, taken in by her beauty.

Somehow he finds it hard to focus when she speaks, and

even though he can't help it, he feels like he must be grinning like an idiot. The woman introduces herself as Rachel and tries to explain what's happened with her car, talking about strange noises and shuddering.

Daniel nods along trying to look sober and wise, and after a few minutes, he follows her out to the car. As he lifts the hood a wave of steam and smoke is released, and Daniel swears as his finger singed. "Sorry, Rachel, I'm ok. It was just the shock of it is all." He smiles sheepishly, trying to keep his cool. "It's ok...Danny" The words sound strange as Rachel says them, and Daniel feels like she's giving him a strange look.

The only thing he can think is that this woman must think he's some weirdo, which is a shame really because Daniel feels like she's the most beautiful woman he's seen in his life. Daniel suppresses a sigh as he leans in under the hood focusing on his work.

The first thing that struck Rachel about the mechanic was his looks. He carried himself with natural confidence and had the kind of looks that Rachel thought you only saw on TV shows. She feels her heart flutter as he stretches out a strong hand, shaking hers. She introduces herself to the Mechanic, who likes to be called Danny, and tries to explain everything that happened to her car.

She feels like she's mumbling like a fool, and seeing Danny smile at her warmly with his strong eyes makes her feel even more self-conscious. She never thought she'd be interested in a mechanic, but as she talks to this man she feels herself blushing like a schoolgirl.

She thinks Danny must be playing it cool because as she talks, he nods and smiles, giving off an air of knowledge. When it comes to fixing the car, Rachel feels her heart jump as Danny gets scalded slightly by the steam from the engine, but he gives her a goofy smile and reassures her before getting back to work.

Rachel thought this day was going bad, but it looks like maybe fate has stepped in after all. Daniel takes a breath and leans back, turning to Rachel. "Well, Rachel," He says in as even a voice as he can manage, "It looks like your engine just overheated."

Rachel frowns, and Daniel can't believe how beautiful she looks even when doing this. "What does that mean, can you fix it?" Daniel gives an apologetic smile. "I've done what I can, but we still need to wait it out until it cools, or you'll just end up like this again." Rachel bites her lip, thinking about lunch.

She definitely can't make it to her usual place to eat, she needs to stay at the garage to watch her car, but they do deliver food. Rachel takes a deep breath and tries to play it casually. "So,

Danny," She says while trying not to blush too hard, "Are you hungry?"

Daniel's schedule has been derailed today, and yet it's the happiest he's been in a long time. When the food first arrived there was an inevitable awkward silence as Rachel and Daniel ate silently, sitting apart. But even that seems like ages ago.

For the past half hour, they've been talking openly, laughing, and sharing stories from their past. Little by little, Daniel and Rachel have nudged and scootched their way nearer to each other, and now they are sitting close together, comfortable, no longer strangers.

Rachel smiles as she finishes the last of her coffee, feeling her leg touch against Daniel's. She can't suppress a blush and, as she places her hand down, trying to remain calm, she feels Daniel's hand slowly drift over as he puts his hand over hers.

Rachel's heart beats faster as she looks over to Daniel, and she sees his cheeks are a bright pink color. "Can I tell you a secret, Rachel? Your car was ready to drive twenty minutes ago. I didn't want to tell you because..then you'd go rushing off, and I might not see you again." Rachel grins at Daniel. "Can I tell you a secret? I'm not completely clueless about cars. ; the uncle was a mechanic. I knew it wouldn't take long to be sorted, that's why Ordered lunch for us, I was hoping you'd be too polite to turn it down." Daniel feels his face break into a grin. "So, are we on the same page here?" Rachel leans in closer, "Let me show you what page I'm on" She says, and At that moment, Rachel pushes close to Daniel, Her hand finding the back of his head, pulling him in for a kiss.

www.ingramcontent.com/pod-product-compliance
Lightning Source LLC
LaVergne TN
LVHW011901060526
838200LV00054B/4458